W9-CDJ-737

Walt Disney's Pinocchio

ADAPTED BY T.J. STEINER

This is the story of Pinocchio. Read along with me. You will know it is time to turn the page when you hear this sound....

One dark night, Jiminy Cricket decided
to take shelter from the rain in a toyshop that was owned
by an old woodcarver named Geppetto. The old man lived
alone with his cat, Figaro, and his goldfish, Cleo.

Jiminy watched Geppetto paint the face on a puppet.

"I have just the name for you," Geppetto said to the
puppet. "Pinocchio!"

"Wouldn't it be nice if he were a real boy?" Geppetto said to Figaro.

Looking out at the Wishing Star, that was exactly the wish Geppetto made.

Sometimes wishes do come true! That night, the beautiful fairy appeared. She touched Pinocchio with her wand.

"Am I a real boy?"
asked the puppet.
"No," the Blue Fairy
said to Pinocchio. Then she
explained that he must prove
himself to be brave, truthful and
unselfish if he were to become a
real boy. She assigned Jiminy to be
his conscience.

After the Blue Fairy disappeared,
Pinocchio danced with glee. His excitement
woke Geppetto, who was overjoyed when he
realized his wish had come true.

The fox and cat sold Pinocchio to Stromboli. Stromboli owned a traveling puppet show, and he put Pinocchio to work. Soon the coins started rolling in.

Pinocchio was delighted with his new fame and fortune. But when the show was over, Stromboli didn't give Pinocchio his share of the gold coins. Instead, Jiminy found Pinocchio locked in a cage!

The Blue Fairy came to Pinocchio's rescue, but he was ashamed to tell her what had really happened.

With every lie his nose got longer and longer and longer! When he finally told the truth, his nose shrank back to normal size and the Blue Fairy helped him escape.

There, in Monstro's belly, Pinocchio found his father.

"Father!" Pinocchio cried.

"Pinocchio! My son!"

There was just one problem: How were they all going to get out of the whale?

Then the little wooden-headed puppet had an idea: Build a fire! The smoke would make the whale sneeze them out.

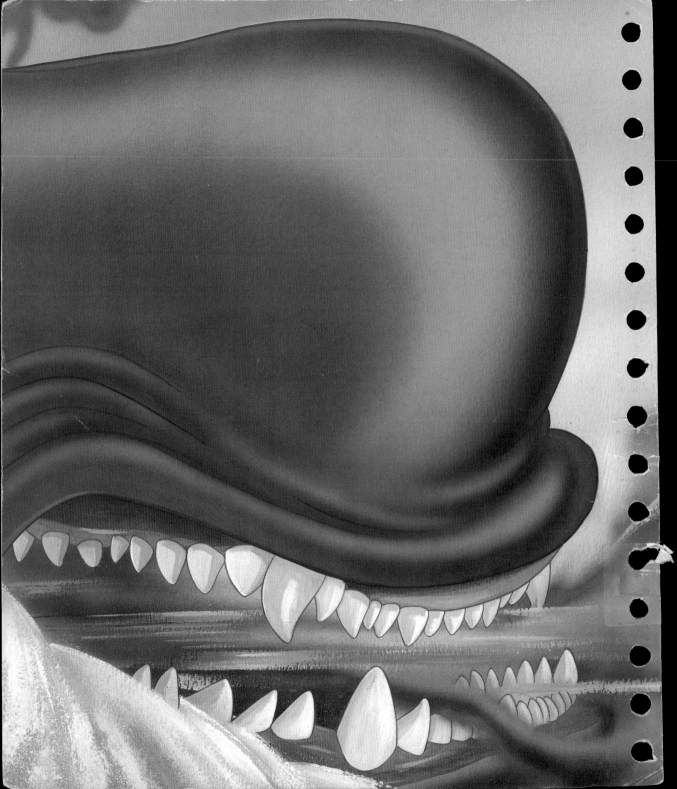

Pinocchio's plan worked! The giant whale sneezed a giant sneeze. Out into the sea they all rushed.

After struggling through wild waves, they washed up onto the shore. Geppetto, Figaro, Cleo and Jiminy were soaked, but safe.

But it didn't look so good for Pinocchio.

Sorrowfully, Geppetto lifted his son in his arms and carried him home.

Pinocchio had proved himself brave, truthful and unselfish.
So the Blue Fairy granted his father's dearest wish.
  "Father!" cried Pinocchio, waking up.
  "You're alive!" cried Geppetto. "And you're a real, live boy!"
  Jiminy smiled. He had been a good conscience, after all.
  And the new family lived happily ever after.